FEB 0 9 2015

Reader's Clubhouse

SAFE STREETS

By Sandy Riggs

Table of Contents

© Copyright 2006 by Barron's Educational Series, Inc.

All inquiries should be addressed to:
Barron's Educational Series, Inc.
250 Wireless Boulevard
Hauppauge, New York 11788
www.barronseduc.com

Library of Congress Control Number: 2005043505

ISBN-13: 978-0-7641-3300-8
ISBN-10: 0-7641-3300-4

Library of Congress Cataloging-In-Publication Data
Riggs, Sandy, 1940–
    Safe Streets / Sandy Riggs.
       p. cm. – (Reader's clubhouse)
    Includes bibliographical references and index.
    ISBN-13: 978-0-7641-3300-8
    ISBN-10: 0-7641-3300-4
    1. City and town life—Juvenile literature. 2. Streets—Juvenile literature. 3. Streets—Maintenance and repair—Juvenile literature. 4. Safety education—Juvenile literature. I. Title. II. Series.

HT152.R54 2006
307.76—dc22

2005043505

PRINTED IN CHINA
9 8 7 6 5 4 3 2 1

Dear Parent and Educator,

Welcome to the Barron's Reader's Clubhouse, a series of books that provide a phonics approach to reading.

Phonics is the relationship between letters and sounds. It is a system that teaches children that letters have specific sounds. Level 1 books introduce the short-vowel sounds. Level 2 books progress to the long-vowel sounds. This progression matches how phonics is taught in many classrooms.

Safe Streets reviews the long-vowel sounds introduced in previous Level 2 books. Simple words with these long-vowel sounds are called **decodable words.** The child knows how to sound out these words because he or she has learned the sounds they include. This story also contains **high-frequency words.** These are common, everyday words that the child learns to read by sight. High-frequency words help ensure fluency and comprehension. **Challenging words** go a little beyond the reading level. The child will identify these words with help from the photograph on the page. All words are listed by their category on page 23.

Here are some coaching and prompting statements you can use to help a young reader read *Safe Streets*:

- **On page 4, "safe" is a decodable word. Point to the word and say:**

  Read this word. How did you know the word? What sounds did it make?

  Note: There are many opportunities to repeat the above instruction throughout the book.

- **On page 16, "workers" is a challenging word. Cover the *-ers* and say:**

  Read this part of the word. (Then show the whole word and say:) *Read the word. How did you know the word? Did you look at the picture? How did it help?*

You'll find more coaching ideas on the Reader's Clubhouse Web site: *www.barronsclubhouse.com.* Reader's Clubhouse is designed to teach and reinforce reading skills in a fun way. We hope you enjoy helping children discover their love of reading!

Sincerely,

Nancy Harris

Nancy Harris
Reading Consultant

We live on a safe street.

We have jobs to keep
the streets safe.

We keep our street clean.

We pick up the trash.

We clear ice from the street.

No one slips and falls
on the street.

Workers paint lines
on our street.

The lines help people stay
in their lanes.

Workers fix the holes
in the street.

Bikes do not bump
over them.

We prune the trees
on the street.

The trees do not hit the lines.

Workers put signs
on the street.

They tell people where to go.

We do a lot to make
a safe street.

What do *you* do to keep *your* street safe?

Fun Facts About
Our Streets

- In 2004, a town in Arizona swept almost 39,000 miles of streets. The result was about 1,700 tons of trash!

- The Great American Cleanup is a nationwide attempt to clean up communities. People choose a date, and volunteers pick up trash, recycle, plant trees, and beautify neighborhoods. In 2003, more than 2 million people in the United States participated.

- You can help keep your street safe by following bicycle-safety rules:

  1. Always ride on the right. Never ride against traffic.
  2. Ride single file.
  3. Stop at all stop signs and street lights.
  4. Always signal before making a turn.

Find Out More

Read a Book

Budd, E. S. *Street Cleaners (Big Machines at Work)*. Child's World, 2000.

Kalman, Bobbie and Niki Walker. *Community Helpers from A to Z* (Alphabasics). Crabtree Publishing Company, 1997.

Visit a Web Site

Community Club
http://teachers.scholastic.com/commclub
Users learn about real-life community workers and their jobs. Of the eight workers discussed, three work to keep our streets safe: utility worker, police officer, and firefighter.

21

Glossary

 **lane** a marked part of a road that keeps traffic in one line

 **prune** to cut branches or twigs from a tree or bush

 **signs** warnings, instructions, or directions you can see

 **trash** garbage or rubbish

Word List

Challenging Words	signs workers	
Decodable Long-Vowel Words	bikes clean clear holes ice keep lanes lines	paint people prune safe stay street streets trees
High-Frequency Words	a and do from go have help in live make no not on one	our over put the their them they to up we what where you your

Index

Photo credits:

Page 4: © Jeff Greenberg/PhotoEdit
Page 7: © Grantpix/Index Stock Imagery
Page 9: © David Young-Wolff/PhotoEdit
Page 10: © Ingram Publishing
Page 12: © Lon C. Diehl/PhotoEdit
Page 13: © Michael Newman/PhotoEdit
Page 15: © Seven Evanston
Page 16: © Dennis MacDonald/PhotoEdit